This Book Is Not for You!

WRITTEN BY
SHANNON HALE

ILLUSTRATED BY
TRACY SUBISAK

DIAL BOOKS FOR YOUNG READERS

Stanley hopped on his bike and zoomed through the cornfield. The bookmobile was waiting at the crossroads, shiny as a rocket ship.

Stanley didn't wait for his bike to
completely stop before he jumped off.
   A book called *The Mysterious
Sandwich* sat up tall on the display
shelf. Stanley liked mysteries, and he
liked sandwiches. Perfect.

MS. CHRISTINE?
CAN I CHECK OUT
THIS BOOK?

A very old man leaned out of the bookmobile.

He read the back of the book, and then
peered at Stanley from beneath his eyebrows.

Stanley really did want to read it,
but now he felt embarrassed.

When Valeria asked for a book, the old man
handed her *The Mysterious Sandwich*.

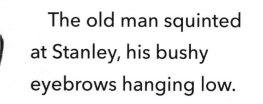

The old man squinted at Stanley, his bushy eyebrows hanging low.

The old man bent over
and peered at the shelves.

AHA! HERE'S A CAT BOOK: *FUZZ, FURR, AND PURR.*

Stanley reached for it, but the old man pulled it back.

NO, I DIDN'T MEAN FOR YOU, YOUNG MAN.

Then for who?

Stanley looked behind him. A tabby cat was padding up to the bookmobile.

He took the book with two furry paws.

HUH.

Stanley smiled. He had to be joking, right?

With a beep and a puff of steam, a robot rolled up to the bookmobile. It checked out the robot book and joined Valeria and the cat on a patch of clover beneath the chestnut tree.

The old man blew his eyebrows out of his eyes.

The old man picked up *Voyage on the Sea of Fire.*

Stanley eyed his bicycle. He wanted to race away as fast as he could and never come back to the bookmobile again.

The old man handed him *The Squelching Peach.*

Stanley sighed, but
he didn't say a word.

The Squelching Peach was kind of funny. Stanley even laughed twice.

Just as he finished
reading it, Valeria closed her book.

Stanley traded her a piece of watermelon gum for a triple mint.

Stanley got so into Valeria's book, he forgot where he was.
He barely even noticed how the breeze crackled in the cornstalks.
Or how much Valeria was laughing at that squelching peach. Or
even that the robot and cat had traded books too.

Stanley didn't look up from his book until heavy footsteps shook the ground and startled the bees to silence. He held his breath. Even the robot's spout stopped steaming.

Trembling, the old man handed over the book.

The allosaurus
propped the book
onto a rock and settled
into the clover.

Stanley stood up, marched over to the bookmobile,
and picked up *Voyage on the Sea of Fire*.

The very old man lifted his enormous eyebrows away from his eyes, and he looked over at a cat reading about robots.

And a robot reading about cats.

An allosaurus reading about ponies, and a girl reading about a peach.

And finally at Stanley.

WELL, I DON'T SEE WHY NOT.

Stanley settled into the crook of the allosaurus's leg and started to read. The cat joined him, and then the robot and Valeria too, all finding comfy reading nooks on the enormous dinosaur.

The allosaurus sighed happily, and everyone who leaned against her couldn't help but rise and fall with her sigh.

The very old man shuffled closer to the pile of readers.

The old man smiled beneath his stormy brows. He settled against the dinosaur and opened a book about goats.

The goat sniffed the book.

The goat snuffled the gum out of
Stanley's hand and began to chew.

PERFECT.

And it was.

FOR CHRISTINE—S.H.

TO ABBY, BENJI, CALEBY, AND DANGEL—T.S.

Dial Books for Young Readers
An imprint of Penguin Random House LLC, New York

First published in the United States of America by Dial Books for Young Readers,
an imprint of Penguin Random House LLC, 2022

Visit us online at penguinrandomhouse.com.

Library of Congress Cataloging-in-Publication Data is available.

Manufactured in Spain
ISBN 9781984816856

2 4 6 8 10 9 7 5 3 1
EST

Design by Jennifer Kelly • Text set in Avenir Next LT Pro and Dreaming Outloud AllCaps

The artwork was created using India ink, Japanese watercolor, pastel, and colored pencil
on Fabriano Artistico watercolor paper.